When Wishes Come True
Text & Illustrations © 2009 Per-Henrik Gürth

Published by Lobster Press™
1620 Sherbrooke Street West, Suites C & D
Montréal, Québec   H3H 1C9
Tel. (514) 904-1100 • Fax (514) 904-1101
www.lobsterpress.com

Publisher: Alison Fripp
Editor: Meghan Nolan
Editorial Assistant: Susanna Rothschild
Graphic Design & Production: Tammy Desnoyers
Consultant on Font & Cover Design: Sara Gillingham
Production Assistant: Leslie Mechanic

We acknowledge the financial support of the Government
of Canada through the Book Publishing Industry
Development Program (BPIDP) for our publishing activities.

The Canada Council | Le Conseil des Arts
for the Arts | du Canada

We acknowledge the support of
the Canada Council for the Arts
for our publishing program.

Library and Archives Canada Cataloguing in Publication

Gürth, Per-Henrik
    When wishes come true / Per-Henrik Gürth.

ISBN 978-1-897550-23-6 (bound).--ISBN 978-1-897550-27-4 (pbk.)

    1. Polar bear--Juvenile fiction.  I. Title.

PS8613.U84W54 2009          jC813'.6          C2009-900034-2

Printed and bound in China.

# When Wishes
# Come True

Per-Henrik Gürth

Lobster Press™

On one bright, clear winter day in the Arctic tundra,
Little Bear was not happy at all.

"What's wrong, my little one?"
Mother Bear asked Little Bear.
"Why aren't you smiling?"

"I would smile if my wishes came true.
But they never do," sighed Little Bear.

"What is it that you wish for?"
asked Mother Bear as she tickled
him under the chin.

"I close my eyes and *I wish and I wish and I wish* I was an astronaut. Then I would fly all the way up to the moon and see the stars up close," said Little Bear. "But when I open my eyes, I see my wish hasn't come true."

"And what else do you wish for?"

"I close my eyes and *I wish and I wish and I wish*
I was a pirate. Then I would sail across the seas
and find deserted islands and hidden treasures,"
Little Bear explained. "But when I open my eyes,
I see my wish hasn't come true."

"Do you have any more wishes?"

"Oh yes," exclaimed Little Bear. "Sometimes I close my eyes and *I wish and I wish and I wish* I was a king.

"Then I would live in a magic castle full of toys and candy and butterflies and chocolate. But when I open my eyes, I see my wish hasn't come true."

"Some wishes might not come true, but many others do," comforted Mother Bear as she put her big arms around him. "You often wish for us to go out at night to gaze at the stars and watch for the northern lights. And we do."

"Yes, I like that very much," Little Bear agreed, smiling a little.

"And sometimes you wish to jump on ice floes, and dive into the sea, and play chase with the belugas," said Mother Bear. "So we do."

"Yes, I really like that," Little Bear nodded, smiling a little more.

"And on many mornings, you wish to have your super-favorite breakfast – codfish with lots of kelp and berries. So I gather that all up for you."

"*Mmmmmmm*, I love my super-favorite breakfast," said Little Bear, licking his lips.

"And sometimes, you wish for the snow to fall so you can catch snowflakes on your tongue and go sledding down the ice packs," said Mother Bear. "So when it snows, that's just what we do."

"Yes, we have so much fun," said Little Bear.

"You are right. Many of my wishes *do* come true!"

"Yes, they do. Sometimes only little wishes come true, but sometimes big wishes too," whispered Mother Bear. "I know this because the biggest wish I've *ever* wished came true."

"Really? What was *your* biggest wish?"

"I closed my eyes and *I wished and I wished and I wished ...*"

"... for *you*."

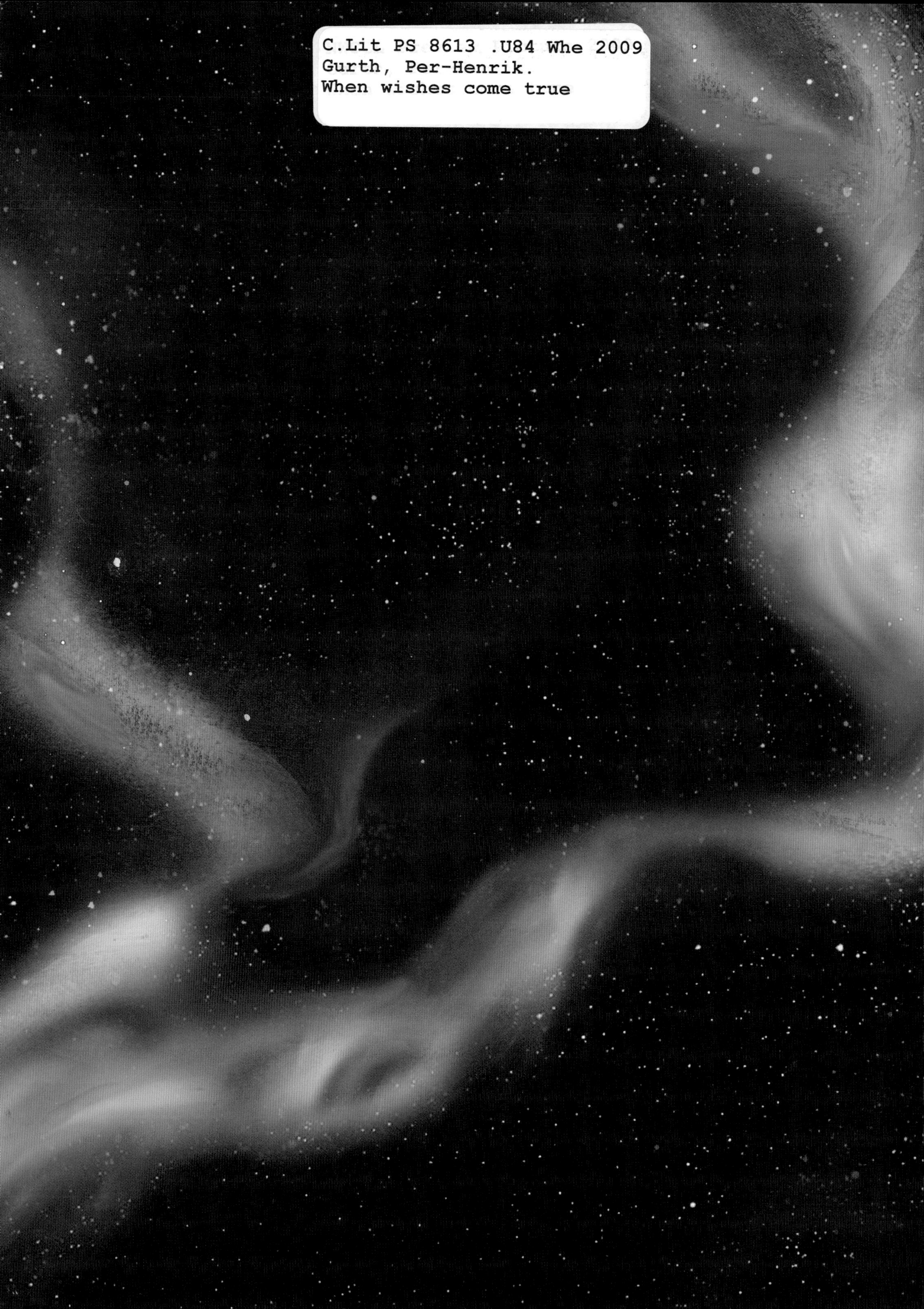